VANISHED!

Kate, Samantha, and Anna were talking in the hall by the water fountain. Their skate bags hung over their shoulders.

"Hurry up, Randi!" Anna shouted. "Your mom is waiting to drive us to the rink."

"Just a minute, girls," Mrs. Griffin said. "Randi can't find her skates."

"*What?*" they all yelled at once.

"Randi! I can't believe it! You lost your skates? What are you going to do?" Anna asked.

"Randi hasn't exactly *lost* her skates," Mrs. Griffin said. "She just doesn't remember where they are right now. Why don't you all check your cubbies? Just in case Randi put her skates in someone else's cubby by mistake."

Anna, Kate, and Samantha emptied their cubbies. They pulled out backpacks, old umbrellas, and library books. But no skates.

Randi felt terrible. Her skates had vanished into thin air! How was she going to win the competition—how was she going to skate at all—without any skates?

Don't miss any of the fun titles in the Silver Blades

FIGURE EIGHTS series!

Randi's Missing Skates

Effin Older

Illustrated by Marcy Ramsey

Created by Parachute Press, Inc.

A SKYLARK BOOK

NEW YORK · TORONTO · LONDON · SYDNEY · AUCKLAND

RL 2.6, 006–009

RANDI'S MISSING SKATES

A Skylark Book / March 1997

Skylark Books is a registered trademark of Bantam Books, a division of Bantam Doubleday Dell Publishing Group, Inc. Registered in U.S. Patent and Trademark Office and elsewhere.

Silver Blades® is a registered trademark of Parachute Press, Inc.

For information address: Bantam Doubleday Dell Books for Young Readers.

ISBN 0-553-48506-7

Published simultaneously in the United States and Canada

Bantam Books are published by Bantam Books, a division of Bantam Doubleday Dell Publishing Group, Inc. Its trademark, consisting of the words "Bantam Books" and the portrayal of a rooster, is Registered in U.S. Patent and Trademark Office and in other countries. Marca Registrada. Bantam Books, 1540 Broadway, New York, New York 10036.

This book is for the Beevers:
Richard, Jeanny, Stephanie, and Rebecca

1

The Competition

Eight-year-old Randi Wong stood in the middle of the rink at the Seneca Hills Ice Arena. Her skating lesson with her club, the Figure Eights, was about to start.

Randi stared down at the shiny gold laces in her skates. The laces were new, but her skates were old. They used to belong to Randi's big sister Jill. Randi didn't mind hand-me-downs. In fact, she loved them.

Jill had given Randi the skates when Randi started lessons with the Figure Eights. Randi still remembered her first time skating with the club. It was the happiest day of her life.

Yesterday had been the *un*happiest day of Randi's life. Yesterday she had found out that Jill was going away again. Far away.

In two weeks Jill was going back to school in Colorado at the International Ice Academy. She would train with some of the best coaches in the world. Jill was going to be a real skating star! She might even be in the Olympics someday!

I'm really going to miss Jill, Randi thought as she glided slowly across the ice. *I wish she didn't have to go to a school so far away.*

Then, behind her, Randi heard giggles. She glanced around. Her good friends Anna Mullen, Kate Alvaro, and Samantha Rivers were skating past her. Anna, Kate, and Samantha belonged to the Figure Eights, too. They were warming up by playing Follow the Leader.

Anna was the leader. She did a bunny hop on the ice. Her brown, curly hair bounced as she landed. Kate and Samantha did bunny hops behind Anna. Then Anna glided on one foot, and Kate and Samantha glided on one foot, too.

I know they're my friends, but I can't tell them how I feel about Jill, Randi decided. *They'll think I'm really dumb. Besides, if I talk about how much I'm going to miss Jill, I might cry. And then I'd be really embarrassed.*

"Earth to Randi! Earth to Randi!"

Randi whirled around.

The Figure Eights' coach, Carol Crandall, skated up to her. "Is your head in the clouds again, Randi?" Carol asked. "I called you three times and you didn't hear me!" She playfully tugged one of Randi's long black braids.

"You'd better finish your warm-up," Carol said. "It's nearly time to start the lesson."

"Okay," Randi said. She turned to skate across the rink. And felt a hard rap on her back. Randi gasped and spun around.

"You're it, Randi!" Woody Bowen yelled. Then he sped off.

"You're it! You're it!" Max Harper and Josh Freeman yelled as they skated past Randi.

Ice tag, Randi realized. *And I'm it!* She took off after Woody. But before she could catch

3

him, Carol reached out and grabbed Woody's big red- and blue-striped shirt.

"Whoa! Not so fast!" Carol called out. "It's time to start."

The members of the Figure Eights all gathered quickly around Carol.

"Everybody's here except Frederika," Kate noticed. She adjusted the red headband in her short blond hair. "Has anyone seen her?"

Samantha pointed across the rink. "There she is."

"Hi!" Frederika waved as she glided up to the group. "Sorry I'm late, Carol," she said to their coach. "I forgot my new sweater at home. I had to go all the way back to get it." Frederika pushed her long blond hair off her shoulder. She twirled around to show off her new pink sweater. "Don't you just *love* it?"

Anna nudged Randi. "All Frederika thinks about is her new sweaters," she whispered.

"I know," Randi agreed. "She must have

more skating sweaters in her closet than your dad has in his whole shop."

Anna's father owned the pro shop at the rink. Many people in Seneca Hills went there to buy skates, leotards, and other skating supplies.

"Okay—we're all here, so listen up," Carol announced. "Next week we're going to have our first-ever competition."

Wow, Randi thought. *A competition! That will be so much fun!*

"Awesome! Who are we skating against?" Woody asked. He turned his blue baseball cap to the back. His messy red hair poked out through the hole in the front.

"Against each other," Carol answered. "I'm going to teach you a short program. It will combine all the moves you've learned so far. Everyone will perform the same program. You can all invite your families and friends. And listen to this—" She paused. Her dark eyes sparkled. "The winner will get a blue ribbon, and their picture will be in the newspaper!"

"Cool!" Randi said.

"Wow!" Kate cried. "I never won anything before!" Then her smile faded. "And I won't this time, either. I always fall. I'm too clumsy to win."

"That makes two of us," Samantha groaned.

Carol put one arm around Kate and the other around Samantha. "Anybody can win," she told them. "But it will take a lot of practice—and concentration." Carol glided to the middle of the ice. "Watch. I'll go through the program."

Randi watched closely.

Carol took off. She skated five long forward strokes, followed by five forward crossovers. Then she turned and skated backward. She did three backward crossovers.

Carol turned forward again. She did a one-foot glide and a bunny hop. *Ooh! That is going to be tricky*, Randi thought. Carol ended the program with an awesome hockey stop. Ice chips sprayed high into the air.

Everybody cheered.

Randi couldn't wait to practice the program. Her first competition! Just like Jill. Jill skated in competitions all the time. Maybe someday Jill and Randi could skate in a competition together! They could be a skating team—the Famous Wong Sisters!

"Wait," Carol called. "There's more!" Everyone stopped and looked at her.

"Jill Wong will be returning to the famous International Ice Academy in Colorado next week," Carol told everyone. "Jill broke her ankle but it's healed now. She'll be going back to study with the best professional skaters."

"Jill's going to be famous someday!" Woody teased.

"Yeah," Anna said. "But Randi, how come you didn't tell us Jill was going back?"

Randi shrugged. "I forgot," she mumbled.

"You forgot something like that?" Anna asked.

Randi shrugged again.

"*Anyway,*" Carol continued, "Jill has agreed

to present the blue ribbon to the winner of our competition, and the winner's picture will be taken *with Jill* for the newspaper."

Me! Randi thought. *It's got to be me! Jill is my big sister! If our picture was in the paper, we really could be the Famous Wong Sisters!*

Then Randi turned to her best friend, Anna. *Oh, no,* Randi thought. She'd just remembered. *Anna is the best skater in Figure Eights.* "You'll win, Anna. I know you will," Randi said.

"Well, I hope I do. But if I don't win, I really want you to, Randi," Anna told her. "It would be totally cool for you and Jill to have your picture taken together for the newspaper."

"I know. Maybe if I try my hardest, I could win," Randi answered. "In fact, I'm going to start right now." She skated off.

Randi started the program just the way Carol did. She did five forward strokes, then the forward crossovers.

All right! Randi thought. *Now for the backward crossovers.*

Randi turned, and caught her skate on an edge in the ice.

Thud! Down she fell.

"Ouch!" Randi yelped. She stood up and brushed ice flakes off her purple tights. *Okay,* she thought. *Again, from the top.*

This time, she turned smoothly into the backward crossovers. But she wobbled on her one-foot glide. Randi stopped and checked to make sure the laces on her skates were tight enough. Carol always said that if your laces were loose, your ankle wouldn't have enough support for a one-foot glide.

Randi bent down over her gold laces. She pulled them to make them tighter and tied the bow again. She straightened up—and saw Anna across the rink.

Randi watched her best friend. Anna moved easily from the one-foot glide to the bunny hop. Then she did a killer hockey stop. Ice chips sprayed everywhere.

Wow! Anna was perfect! Even in the hardest parts! Randi thought.

"Excellent, Anna!" Carol called from the side of the ice. "Good job!"

Anna is really good, Randi thought. *And if I'm going to win this competition and get my picture in the paper, I'll have to beat Anna. How am I ever going to do that?*

2

The Famous Wong Sisters

That afternoon Randi hurried upstairs to her room. She tossed her backpack onto her bed and pulled open her closet door.

I've got to find that T-shirt. Anna and I planned to wear our matching purple panda T-shirts on Friday, Randi thought.

"Where *is* it?" Randi muttered. "I know it's here somewhere."

Randi went through the big pile of clothes on her closet floor. She tossed T-shirts, pants, and skirts everywhere. No purple shirt. Then she searched her bureau drawers. Still no shirt. "Where could it be?" she said out loud.

11

"Hey, Mom!" she called. "Have you seen my purple panda T-shirt?"

"No, Randi," Mrs. Wong called back from the kitchen.

Randi moaned. "I looked *everywhere,* and I can't find it! Can you come help me?" she called to her mother.

Mrs. Wong jogged up the stairs. As she entered Randi's room, she groaned. "This room is a mess! No wonder you have been losing things lately. Like your panda shirt—and your dinosaur book. No one could find *anything* in here, Randi! This is a disaster!"

Randi looked around. *Mom's right,* she admitted to herself. *My room* is *a disaster!*

"Some of this stuff is Laurie's," Randi mumbled. "She makes the room messy, too." Laurie was Randi's three-year-old sister. Laurie and Randi shared the room.

"Don't blame Laurie," Mrs. Wong said. "You're eight years old—old enough to be responsible for your things and to keep your room neat. And that's exactly what I want you to do. Start right now. I want you to have this room clean before dinner."

"But, Mom, I'll never get it done before dinner!" Randi argued.

Mrs. Wong put her hands on her hips.

Uh-oh, Randi thought. *Mom is really serious.*

Randi sighed. "Okay, I'll do it," she said.

Mrs. Wong went downstairs. Randi kicked one of Laurie's stuffed animals over to Laurie's side of the room. Then she began to pick up her own things.

Randi scooped up four pairs of socks from a pile of clothes on the floor. Then she picked up a blue T-shirt, a pink sweater, and her orange tights.

She stopped short. Something fell from underneath her tights. Randi bent down. What was it? Randi found her favorite detective book, *Sally Smith, Super Detective, and the Case of the Missing Letter.*

"I thought I lost this book! I've been looking all over for it!" Randi said out loud. She plopped down on the pile of clothes and opened the book. Her bookmark was still inside!

Randi started reading on page six. Sally Smith was working on a big case. She had to find out who stole an important letter from the president of the United States! Sally searched for clues using a magnifying glass. She also took notes with a special pad and pen.

Randi and all her friends loved reading about Sally Smith, Super Detective. "I'll just read one or two pages," Randi told herself. "Then I'll finish cleaning my room."

But Randi didn't stop. She read and read. Then she heard her mother calling, "Randi! Dinner!"

Randi shut the book. Her room was still a total mess. *Oh, no!* she thought. *Maybe Mom forgot all about telling me to clean my room.*

Randi hurried into the dining room. She slid into her usual chair beside Jill. She glanced around the table at her big, noisy family.

Randi's six-year-old twin brothers, Michael and Mark, were at one end of the table. They were having a scary face contest. They growled and yelled and made faces at each other while they sat in their seats.

Laurie screamed, too, and waved her arms. She knocked over her glass of milk. Mr. Wong leaped up from his chair and wiped up the spill.

Jill had a skating magazine opened at her place and was reading. Ten-year-old Kristi was arguing loudly with their older brother, Henry, who was twelve.

For once Randi was glad everyone was so noisy.

Mrs. Wong carried a tray of food in from the kitchen. "Randi, did you finish cleaning your room?" she asked.

Randi's face turned red. "Not yet, Mom," she admitted. "It's a big job. I'll finish after dinner. Promise."

"Randi—" Mrs. Wong began.

"Really, Mom," Randi said. "I promise. I have to wear my purple panda shirt to school on Friday. And I still haven't found it!"

Randi leaned across the table toward Kristi. "Do you have my purple shirt?" Randi asked.

"Nope," Kristi answered. "But you still have my library book on jungle animals, don't you?"

"I—I think so," Randi stammered.

"Well, I need it back," Kristi said. "I hope you didn't lose it, the same way you lost your dinosaur book last week. You must owe tons of money. It's been overdue for a week!"

"Honestly, Randi," Mrs. Wong said. "You have been losing too many things lately. You need to be more responsible. We can't afford to replace everything you lose. You are going to have to pay your overdue fines from your own allowance."

Randi looked down at her plate. "Okay, Mom. I'll be more careful from now on. I promise." Then she turned to Henry. "Have *you* seen my purple shirt?"

"Which purple shirt?" Henry asked.

"The one with the panda on the back," Randi said.

"Yeah, I've seen it," Henry told her.

"You *have*?" Randi asked. "Great!"

"Uh-huh," Henry went on, "I thought it was a rag. I used it to polish my bike."

"What!" Randi squealed. "You used my brand-new shirt—"

"Henry! Stop teasing Randi!" Jill said sharply.

Henry flashed a big smile at Randi. "Just kidding."

Randi felt her face turn red with anger. Henry *always* teased her. And she *always* fell for it. "Dirt ball!" Randi muttered. She glared at her brother.

"Hey! Who are you calling a dirt ball?" Henry shouted back. "You're the one with the sloppy room!"

"Okay, you two," Mr. Wong broke in, "no fighting at the dinner table."

Randi stuck her tongue out at Henry.

"Randi!" Mr. Wong scolded. Then he changed the subject. "Tell us how your Figure Eights lesson was today."

Randi burst into a big smile. "Listen, everybody—Figure Eights is having its first-ever skating competition! The winner gets a blue ribbon—and their picture in the newspaper *with Jill*!"

"That's my news, too," Jill said, smiling at Randi. "Randi's coach asked me to present the blue ribbon to the winner of her competition. She said I would inspire all the Figure Eights."

"Wouldn't it be great if *I* won the ribbon?" Randi asked her sister. "Then you could give it to me—and *our* picture would be in the newspaper."

"That would be *totally* cool," Jill agreed. "Hey! That reminds me!" She pushed her chair away from the table and dashed upstairs. In a minute she was back. She held out a page neatly cut from a newspaper.

"That's me, when I won *my* first blue ribbon," Jill said. "And look—I'm wearing the skates I gave *you*, Randi."

Randi stared at the photograph. *Jill won her first competition,* she thought. *And now she's a great skater! If I win my first competition, I'll*

be a great skater, too. Then someday Jill and I will be the Famous Wong Sisters.

"You just do your best in the competition, Randi," Mrs. Wong said. "That's all we want."

"Yeah, but it *would* be awesome if you won, like Jill," Kristi added.

Mr. Wong reached over and ruffled Randi's hair. "We will all be proud of Randi—win or lose!" he declared.

Randi smiled up at her big sister. "Don't worry, everyone. I'll do my best. To win—just like Jill."

3

The Backpack Mystery

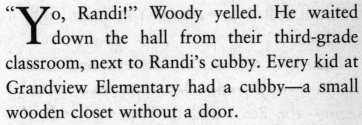

"Yo, Randi!" Woody yelled. He waited down the hall from their third-grade classroom, next to Randi's cubby. Every kid at Grandview Elementary had a cubby—a small wooden closet without a door.

Randi waved, and hurried toward Woody. She wore her blue jeans and a red T-shirt. She hadn't been able to find her purple panda T-shirt. Randi hoped Anna wouldn't be mad at her for not wearing it.

Randi also hadn't finished cleaning her room. She hoped her mom would be too busy today to notice. Randi promised herself she would clean her room by the end of this weekend.

It was Friday morning. All day Wednesday and Thursday Randi thought about the competition, about *winning* the competition, and about her and Jill becoming the Famous Wong Sisters.

"Hurry up! Gym class starts in two minutes!" Woody shouted. He made a fist. "We're going to crush the Tigers!"

Randi rolled her eyes. "You mean, they'll crush *us*."

Their gym teacher, Ms. Stevens, had divided Randi's third-grade class into two kickball teams—the Bears and the Tigers. Randi and Woody played for the Bears. So did Josh, Kate, and Samantha.

So far, the Bears had lost every single game to the Tigers.

"Race you to the playground!" Woody yelled. He took off down the hallway. Randi carefully slid her backpack off. It was extra-fat this morning. Besides Randi's schoolbooks and pencils, it was stuffed with shells and textbooks for her science project on the ocean.

Most important, Randi carried her skates in her backpack. She slid it carefully into her cubby. Then she sprinted to the playground after Woody.

The Bears and the Tigers were gathered around Ms. Stevens. Randi stood close to Woody and Kate.

"Okay, teams," Ms. Stevens called. "We have time to play three innings. The Tigers are up first."

Everyone took their places. Randi ran to third base and the game started.

In the first inning, the Tigers kicked *three* home runs. Randi thought the Bears were about to be crushed—again. But then, in the second inning, Woody, Kate, Josh, and Samantha each scored a run. For the first time ever, the Bears were ahead—4 to 3!

In the third and final inning the Bears were still in the lead. It was the Tigers' turn to kick the ball. The Bears were in the field. "Let's go, Bears!" Randi cheered.

Josh rolled the ball and got the first player out. Then Samantha tagged the second player out.

Yes! One more out and we'll finally win! Randi thought excitedly.

Then Jessica Lind stepped up to the plate.

Oh, no! Randi thought. *Jessica is the Tigers' best player. We'll never get her out!*

Josh rolled the ball to Jessica. Jessica kicked it. Hard. The ball bounced once and flew straight at Randi. Jessica raced to first.

"Get it, Randi!" Woody shouted from the outfield.

Randi held her arms out to catch the ball. Jessica sprinted to second base.

"Home run! Home run!" the Tigers chanted.

Randi's heart pounded wildly. She had to catch the ball! If she did, she could tag Jessica out! And the Bears would finally beat the Tigers!

Jessica flew toward third base. The ball slid

into Randi's arms. She held on to it and twirled around to tag Jessica.

Slam!

Randi crashed into Jessica. Jessica toppled and fell right on her bottom. But Randi held on to the ball!

"Jessica is out!" Ms. Stevens shouted.

"Yay! We won!" the Bears screamed.

Randi reached out a hand toward Jessica. "Are you okay?" she asked.

"Why did you do that?" Jessica shrieked.

"Do what?" Randi asked.

Jessica's face turned red. "Why did you knock me down? You did it on purpose!" she yelled.

"I did *not* knock you down on purpose," Randi declared.

"Yes, you did! You pushed me down so the Bears would win!" Jessica yelled. She stood up and brushed off her T-shirt. "You're a big cheat, Randi!"

Before Randi could say another word, Jessica stormed off the playground.

The Bears crowded around Randi. They whooped and yelled and high-fived each other.

"Good play, Randi!" Woody yelled.

"Way cool," Kate added. "But what's with Jessica?"

Randi sighed. "She said I pushed her down on purpose."

"You did not!" Samantha declared. "She's just mad because the Tigers lost. And *we* won!" Samantha grabbed Randi's hand. "Come on. Don't worry about Jessica. Let's go change, or we'll be late getting back to class."

Randi raced back inside with her friends. She spotted Jessica down the hall—right by Randi's cubby.

"What's she doing over there?" Randi wondered out loud.

Woody frowned. "What are you talking about?"

"There's Jessica, standing by *my* cubby," Randi said again. "What is she up to over there?"

Then Jessica's friend Lisa walked by. She

27

stopped to talk to Jessica. And the two of them walked into their classroom together.

"Looks like she was waiting for Lisa," Woody answered.

"Right," Randi said. She could feel her face turning red with embarrassment.

Randi and Woody walked into the classroom and took their seats.

"Everyone take out your math homework," Mrs. Griffin instructed.

Randi shuffled through the things in her desk. She had notebooks, crumpled-up papers, and stale cookie crumbs.

But no math homework.

Randi groaned. *Oh, no. I must have left my homework in my cubby.* She raised her hand high. "Mrs. Griffin," she called, "I forgot my homework. It's in my cubby. May I go get it?"

"Okay, Randi," Mrs. Griffin answered. "But please hurry."

Randi dashed to her cubby. She pulled out her backpack and peered inside.

"Where is that math homework?" she muttered. "It's got to be here somewhere."

She reached into the backpack and found the bag of seashells she had collected for her science project. Then there were the three textbooks on ocean life.

Randi reached down farther. She felt her pencil case and her book about Sally Smith, Super Detective. Finally, she felt some loose papers and carefully pulled them out.

"Yes!" she exclaimed. "My math homework!" She ran back toward her classroom.

Wait a minute. Randi stopped. *Something's wrong. Something's missing!*

She raced back to her cubby. She took out her backpack and dumped it onto the floor.

Seashells, her books, and her pencil case tumbled out along with a roll of peppermint candies and some crumpled-up tissues.

Oh, no! she thought.

She peered inside the backpack—it was completely empty.

"No!" she cried. "My skates! They're gone!"

4

The First Clue

Randi couldn't believe it! Where were her skates?

I was in a hurry when I left for school this morning, she thought. *But I always put my skates in the bottom of my backpack. I'm sure I took them with me.*

She thought hard. They were her special skates—Jill's old skates. She would never forget them.

So where were they?

Randi rushed back to class. Mrs. Griffin was waiting at the door. "What took you so long, Randi?" she asked.

"Sorry, Mrs. Griffin," Randi managed to mutter.

"It's okay," Mrs. Griffin said. "Take your seat and we'll go over the homework."

Randi's math homework was fine, but all day, she couldn't stop worrying about her skates.

When the bell rang at the end of the day, Randi stood in front of Mrs. Griffin's desk.

Mrs. Griffin glanced up from her work. She noticed Randi's sad face. "What's wrong, Randi?" she asked.

"I put my skates in my backpack this morning, and now they're gone!" Randi answered. "I searched everywhere in my cubby. But I can't find them." Randi felt tears well up in her eyes.

Mrs. Griffin patted Randi's hand. "Calm down, now. I'm sure they didn't just get up and walk away. Or should I say, *skate* away?"

Randi was too upset to smile at Mrs. Griffin's joke.

Mrs. Griffin stood up from her desk. "Come

on. Let's look around together." She took Randi's hand and led her out of the classroom.

Kate, Samantha, and Anna were talking in the hall by the water fountain. Their skate bags hung over their shoulders.

"Hurry up, Randi!" Anna shouted. "Your mom is waiting to drive us to the rink."

"Just a minute, girls," Mrs. Griffin said. "Randi can't find her skates."

"*What?*" they all yelled at once.

"Randi! I can't believe it! You lost your skates? What are you going to do?" Anna asked.

"Randi hasn't exactly *lost* her skates," Mrs. Griffin said. "She just doesn't remember where they are right now. Why don't you all check your cubbies? Just in case Randi put her skates in someone else's cubby by mistake."

Anna, Kate, and Samantha emptied their cubbies. They pulled out backpacks, old umbrellas, and library books. But no skates.

Randi felt terrible. Her skates had vanished into thin air! How was she going to win the

competition—how was she going to skate at all—without any skates?

"Have you forgotten how to do the bunny hop?" Carol asked Randi later that afternoon. "You took so many falls today. And your one-foot glide was wobbly. Are you feeling okay?"

"I'm fine," Randi answered. "It's just my unlucky day." She smiled to hide how terrible she really felt.

Randi was wearing borrowed skates at practice. Mr. Mullen had loaned her a pair from the Lost and Found at the pro shop. And they were too big!

Randi didn't want to tell Carol why she was wobbling and falling at practice. She couldn't admit that she had lost her skates. What if Carol told Randi's mom about it? Mrs. Wong was already angry with Randi for losing things—and for not cleaning her room.

Mom would be furious if she knew I lost my only pair of skates, Randi thought. *I have to find them before the competition. That way*

Mom will never have to know they were miss-ing! But how?

"The competition is in a week," Carol told Randi. "Try to get in some serious practice be-fore then."

"I will," Randi replied. *As soon as I get my skates back,* she added to herself. *I have to think of a way to find them. And fast!*

Soon Randi had an idea. After practice she found Anna, Kate, and Samantha in the locker room, changing into their sneakers.

"I need your help," Randi told them. "You have to help me find my skates!"

"We'll do anything," Anna said. Samantha nodded.

"What's the plan?" Kate asked.

"It's really cool," Randi said. "I got it from a Sally Smith, Super Detective, story I'm reading. It's called *The Case of the Missing Letter*." Randi stepped closer to Anna, Kate, and Sa-mantha.

"In the story, Sally Smith looks for clues to help her find a letter," Randi explained.

"That's my plan—to look for clues to find my skates."

"Great idea!" Samantha clapped her hands in excitement. "I love playing detective. Have *you* found any clues?"

Randi shook her head. "Nope. I haven't started looking yet." She glanced at her friends. "Can you guys think of a way to find some?"

Everybody thought hard for a minute.

"Sally Smith, Super Detective, always looks for strange and unusual things," Anna said. "Did you see anything strange or unusual today, Randi?"

Randi wrinkled her brow. "I don't think so. I was too worried about my skates to—" She stopped. "Yes! I *did* see something strange. I saw Jessica hanging around my cubby after the kickball game."

"Could that be a clue?" Anna asked everyone.

"Hey!" Samantha cried. "Jessica was really mad at you during kickball today! She thought

36

you knocked her down on purpose. Remember?"

"Yes," Randi answered. "What does that have to do with anything?"

"What if Jessica took your skates?" Samantha said.

"Wait," Randi told her. "Why would Jessica want my skates? She can get her own."

"Jessica was really mad at you, right?" Kate asked. "Maybe she wanted to get back at you."

"You're right!" Randi felt a burst of excitement. "Jessica might want to get back at me for knocking her down. But now we need *proof*—some way to show that *only* Jessica could have taken my skates."

The four girls thought for another minute. No one said anything.

Finally Randi stood up. "My mom's picking me up in a few minutes," she told her friends. "I'd better take these skates back to the Lost and Found before she gets here."

Randi picked up the borrowed skates and

started out of the locker room. Everyone followed behind her.

Randi took two steps into the lobby. She stopped short and gasped. She couldn't believe what she saw!

5

A Clue!

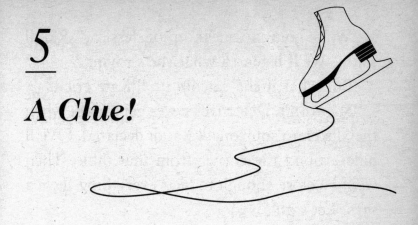

"Look!" Randi whispered to her friends. "There's Jessica!"

She pointed across the lobby of the ice rink.

Jessica stood with her mother in front of a table. A sign taped to the front of the table read, SIGN UP FOR LESSONS HERE!

"What's Jessica doing at the ice rink?" Anna asked.

Randi narrowed her eyes. "I don't know," she answered. "But we have to find out. Come on!"

"Where are we going?" Kate asked.

"We're going to sneak up on Jessica," Randi said. "We'll listen to what she's saying."

"But what if she catches us?" Kate cried.

"She won't. Detectives never get caught when they listen to someone," Randi declared. "We'll hide around the corner from that table. Then we'll be close enough to hear everything Jessica says. Let's go!"

Randi tiptoed silently across the lobby. Anna, Kate, and Samantha followed.

Randi crouched next to the wall. She peeked around the corner at Jessica. "This is the perfect spot," she told her friends. "We can see *them,* but they can't see *us.*"

"This is so exciting!" Samantha whispered. "Just like in the movies!"

Randi put her fingers to her lips. "Shhh. Listen!"

"Happy birthday, honey," Randi heard Mrs. Lind say.

"This is the best birthday present in the whole wide world, Mom!" Jessica shouted. "Thanks! I can't wait to go to my first lesson."

Mrs. Lind turned to the lady behind the table. "When did you say the club meets?" she asked.

"Every Tuesday and Friday afternoon. Jessica is signed up for the next group of sessions," the lady answered.

Anna poked Randi in the side. "Randi! Jessica is signing up for lessons every Tuesday and Friday afternoon," Anna whispered. "That's when we have our Figure Eights lessons!"

The lady ran her finger down a list of numbers. "The lessons are sixty dollars."

"Sixty dollars!" Samantha whispered. "That's how much our Figure Eights lessons cost!"

"I can't believe it!" Randi said quietly. "Jessica's signing up for skating lessons with the Figure Eights! Now we have proof! Jessica took my skates because she needed them for skating lessons!"

"That's silly," Kate told Randi. "Jessica doesn't need *your* skates to take lessons in. She can get her own pair. A new pair. Jessica signed up for lessons, but that doesn't prove she took your skates at all!"

Randi frowned. Kate was right.

Anna stood up and narrowed her eyes at Jessica. "Well, I *still* think Jessica took your skates, Randi. I'm going to make her give them back to you right now!" Anna stepped out from behind the wall.

"Wait!" Randi cried. She pulled Anna back by her T-shirt. "*I* think Jessica is the thief," Randi told Anna. "And *you* think Jessica is the thief. But are you *sure*?"

Anna stared at Randi. "I . . . I *think* so."

Randi shook her head. "*Think* isn't good enough. We have to *know*. We can't tell Jessica to give back the skates. Not until we're totally sure that she took them. We have to *prove* it."

"That sounds right," Samantha agreed. "That's what Sally Smith, Super Detective, would do."

"No problem," Kate said. "We'll just collect evidence to prove that Jessica's the thief."

"Right!" Anna agreed. "Anybody know how to do that?" she asked.

"I do," Randi said. A grin spread across her face.

Her friends moved closer to her. "We'll start on Monday, and we'll get everyone to help," Randi explained. "We'll all follow Jessica at school. We'll watch her every minute and never let her out of our sight. Pretty soon she'll make a mistake that will lead us to my skates!"

Randi's dark eyes sparkled with excitement. "And I'll have my skates back in time for the competition!"

6

Randi Wong, Super Detective

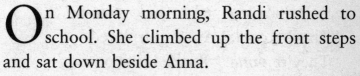

On Monday morning, Randi rushed to school. She climbed up the front steps and sat down beside Anna.

"I can't wait to start spying on Jessica!" Randi cried. "I brought all sorts of detective gear and—"

"Shhh!" Anna poked Randi. "Look who's coming."

Randi turned. *Jessica!*

She hurried up the school steps straight toward Anna and Randi. But as she came closer, Jessica tripped! She dropped her backpack. Everything inside it spilled out onto the steps.

Randi watched as Jessica quickly gathered everything back together. She caught a glimpse of something glittering in the sunlight.

"Look at that!" Randi whispered to Anna.

"Look at what?" Anna asked.

"Look at what fell out of Jessica's bag!" Randi told her.

A pair of *gold shoelaces* lay on the concrete steps. Jessica stooped to pick them up.

"They're cool," Anna murmured.

"They're *mine*!" Randi burst out.

"What do you mean?" Anna asked.

"I had gold laces exactly like those in my missing skates!" Randi told Anna.

Anna's eyes widened in surprise.

Randi jumped up and marched over to Jessica. "Where did you get those gold shoelaces?" Randi demanded.

Jessica stared at Randi. She glanced down at the laces in her hand. Then she looked back up at Randi. "That's none of your business," she snapped. She stomped past Randi and disappeared through the front door.

"Wow!" Anna exclaimed. "She wouldn't tell you where she got the laces!"

"I know. And I think it's because she took them from me," Randi said. "But that still isn't proof."

"It isn't?" Anna asked.

"No," Randi had to admit. "I guess Jessica could have bought a pair of gold laces herself. It's not like we found her with the *skates*. *That* would be proof."

"Hi, Randi! Hi, Anna!" Kate and Samantha called. They walked up the school steps. Josh and Woody followed right behind them.

"Hey! Check out my new puppets!" Woody shouted. He held up four fingers. On the end of each finger was the top half of a peanut shell with a face drawn on it.

"Meet Joe, Joe-Bill, Joe-Bob, and Joe-Bud," Woody said. He wriggled one finger as he said each puppet's name.

Everybody laughed.

Anna stuck her nose up close to one of the puppets. "Are you good at finding evidence, Joe-Bob?"

"Evidence for what?" Joe-Bob asked in a squeaky Woody voice.

"Evidence to prove that Jessica took Randi's skates," Anna answered.

Woody's finger wriggled. "Just call me Joe-Bob, the Great Skate Detective," the peanut shell answered.

Everybody laughed again.

Randi filled Woody and Josh in on what had happened since her skates vanished.

"And this morning Jessica came to school with *gold laces* hidden in her backpack," Anna added. "Just like the ones in Randi's skates!"

"We think she's the thief," Randi told them. "But we have to prove it. Will you guys help us?"

"Sure!" Woody and Josh cried. "What do you want us to do?"

Randi told them her plan. "Today we'll *tail* Jessica. That means we'll follow her everywhere. We won't let her out of our sight. We'll watch her every move. If she does anything strange, write it down. We'll meet after school to report on what we found. Got it?"

"Got it!" Woody and Josh said.

Woody held up his finger puppets. "I bet we'll catch the thief by the end of the day. Right, guys?"

All four fingers wriggled. "Right!" the peanut shells squealed in Woody's voice.

Everyone moved toward the doors to go inside.

"Wait!" Randi yelled. "I almost forgot. I brought some detective equipment for everyone to use!"

Randi reached into her pocket. She pulled out six small notebooks and pens, a magnifying glass, and a funny, floppy brown hat. She handed out notebooks and pens to everyone. She handed Josh the magnifying glass. She kept the brown hat for herself.

"What's the hat for?" Woody asked.

"It's my disguise," Randi explained. She

pulled the hat onto her head. It was so big, it covered her eyes.

Woody laughed. "Awesome! I would never know it was you, Randi!"

The bell rang.

"Good luck spying!" Anna called. She raced to her fourth-grade classroom. The others scrambled into their third-grade classroom.

Randi took her seat and removed her hat. *It will be easy for us to keep track of Jessica,* she thought. *She sits right in the front row!*

Randi and her friends tailed Jessica all day.

When Jessica went to the back of the room, Randi went to the back of the room.

When Jessica fed the pet gerbils, Samantha fed the pet gerbils.

When Jessica went to the bathroom, Kate went to the bathroom, too.

Randi glanced around the classroom at her friends. She saw Woody scribbling in his detective notebook. Josh was peering at Jessica through the magnifying glass.

Randi hoped they would have enough evidence to find her skates before the end of the day!

After lunch Mrs. Griffin announced that everyone could go to the library. Each person would get a turn. "Who would like to go first?" she asked.

Jessica's hand shot up.

"Okay, Jessica. You may go," Mrs. Griffin said. "I'll expect you back with your book in five minutes." Jessica nodded and headed for the door. She left the classroom.

Oh, no! Randi thought. *I can't lose sight of Jessica! I have to follow her!*

Randi raised her hand. "Uh, Mrs. Griffin," she called. "I would like to go to the library now, too. May I?"

"I suppose," Mrs. Griffin answered, "but remember, you're there to pick out a book—not to talk to Jessica."

"No problem, Mrs. Griffin," Randi called back as she bolted out of the classroom.

Randi ran into the hall. Jessica was there, but

she wasn't headed to the library. She was going to her cubby!

She's not supposed to be going to her cubby now! Randi thought. *This is very strange.*

Randi moved to her own cubby, which was across the hall from Jessica's. She pretended to search for something inside. All the time, she sneaked looks at Jessica.

What if Jessica hid my skates in her cubby? Randi wondered.

Just then, Jessica left her cubby. She headed toward the library.

Now is my chance to do some real *super-snooping,* Randi thought. She raced across the hall to Jessica's cubby.

If my skates are in here, I'm going to find them. Right now! she thought.

She peered into Jessica's cubby. Jessica's sweater was hung neatly on one hook. Her baseball mitt hung on the other hook. Jessica's backpack sat on the bottom of the cubby. Randi stared at it. The backpack was open!

Randi checked out the hall. It was empty. No

one was coming. Randi quickly bent down and leaned close to Jessica's backpack. She peeked inside.

The backpack held a notebook, and the gold laces Randi had seen earlier. Otherwise, it was empty. Randi's skates weren't there!

Where did Jessica put them? Randi wondered.

She stood up and turned toward the library. She heard her classroom door swing open.

"Randi!" Mrs. Griffin called. "What are you still doing in the hall? Why aren't you at the library?"

Randi felt her cheeks flush bright red. "Uh— I'm going to the library—right now, Mrs. Griffin."

Mrs. Griffin frowned. "I want you and Jessica to be back here—with books—in exactly three minutes."

"Okay, Mrs. Griffin," Randi said. She raced to the library.

Randi frowned as she ran. There was no evidence at all in Jessica's cubby.

What if I never prove that Jessica is the thief? she wondered. *Even worse, what if I never find my skates?*

When school was out that afternoon, Randi led everybody to the far corner of the playground. She had to be sure that nobody could hear what they were saying.

"So, did you discover any clues?" Randi asked everyone excitedly. "Did you see Jessica do anything strange or unusual? Anything that might lead us to my skates?"

Josh spoke first. "I followed her to the water fountain three times. Twice in the morning and once in the afternoon. She seems *really* thirsty. That's unusual."

"What's unusual about that?" Woody asked. "Maybe she ate salty food for lunch. Salty food always makes me thirsty."

"Well, I followed Jessica to the bathroom," Kate reported. "She stayed in there ten whole minutes—just brushing her hair."

Woody wrinkled his brow. "That's not so

strange," he told Kate. "Lots of girls spend hours brushing their hair!"

Randi turned to Woody. "Well, did *you* see Jessica do anything strange today?"

"*Did* I!" Woody cried. He pulled out his detective notebook and flipped through the pages. "First, I showed Jessica my finger puppets. She didn't think they were cool at all. Then I told her my funniest knock-knock joke. And she didn't laugh!"

Anna raised her eyebrows. "But Woody, some of your jokes *aren't* funny," she said.

"Yeah, and maybe Jessica doesn't *like* finger puppets," Samantha added.

"Don't you have any more evidence?" Randi asked.

"Sure!" Woody replied. "I saw her put the paint jars back where the glue jars go after we had art today. And she asked to help clean up! Nobody ever asks to clean up," Woody said. He crossed his arms over his chest. "I think that's totally strange *and* unusual."

Randi groaned. "Guys, none of that stuff is

evidence. None of it proves that Jessica is the thief!"

"Well, what about you, Randi?" Kate asked. "Did *you* find any evidence?"

"No. Nothing at all," Randi answered. She looked at her friends. "Thanks, guys. You did good detective work. But we still have a major problem." She sighed. "We still didn't prove that Jessica stole my skates. And if we can't prove it, how will I *ever* get them back?"

7

Randi's Big Crash!

"**W**ant a French fry?" Anna asked Randi. They sat with Woody on the bleachers at the Seneca Hills Ice Arena. "I covered them in ketchup, just the way you love them."

"Nah, I don't feel like eating," Randi answered.

"I'll eat your share," Woody offered. He popped a gooey fry into his mouth.

"Go ahead," Randi mumbled. She cupped her chin in her hands and stared gloomily down at the ice. Jill was there, practicing with her skating club, Silver Blades.

Jill had brought Randi to the rink after

Randi's detective meeting. Randi didn't have a lesson with Figure Eights today, but she was still going to spend the afternoon at the rink, watching Jill practice. She spent most afternoons there.

Anna and Woody were also watching the Silver Blades practice. They were always at the rink, too. Anna stayed while her dad ran the pro shop. Woody stayed while his mother worked in her office. She was the president of Silver Blades, and she always had phone calls to make and letters to write.

"I can't believe you're turning down French fries," Anna said. "What's up?"

"I feel sick," Randi explained.

"Not the stinky, throw-up kind of sick, I hope," Woody said. He scooted down to the next bleacher.

"No. I'm not going to *be* sick. I just *feel* sick because I haven't found my skates yet," Randi told him. She groaned. "If we don't find them soon, I'm going to have to tell my mom. She'll be furious! Plus, tomorrow's our last practice before the competition! I need to go over the program in *my* skates!"

"Don't worry, Randi," Woody said, licking ketchup off his fingers. "I just know we'll find your skates in time."

"Sure we will," Anna added.

Randi knew her friends were trying to cheer her up. But there was only one way she *could* cheer up—she had to find her skates.

"Are you sure you can't skate today?" Randi asked Kate the next afternoon. "It's your last chance to practice for the competition."

Kate moaned. She sat on a bench in the locker room and hugged her stomach. "I know I should practice," she said. "But I can't. That last slice of pizza did it. I'm stuffed full of pepperoni!"

"Well then, thanks for letting me borrow your skates," Randi said.

Even though Randi still didn't have her

skates back, she decided to try her hardest today. She could still practice for the competition in case she *did* find her skates.

Randi loosened the laces and squeezed one foot into Kate's skate. "Yikes! This really pinches!" she said. She squashed her other foot into the other skate. "Whoa! This one's even tighter!" Randi said.

"Are they too tight for practice?" Kate asked.

"Nah," Randi replied. "They'll be great." She winced in pain as she stood up. "No one will ever guess they're not mine."

Randi made her way slowly out to the ice. She tried not to show how much her feet hurt. The rest of the Figure Eights were already warming up. Carol skated over to her.

"Take a few minutes to warm up," she told Randi. "Then we'll all run through the program together."

Randi stepped onto the ice. She tried to skate forward, but her skates were so tight, she couldn't even glide. All she could do was take teeny-tiny steps. Like a baby. She hoped no-body would notice.

"What's the matter, Randi? You're skating funny!" Woody yelled as he sped past her.

Randi felt her face grow hot.

Uh-oh. Woody noticed. What if Carol notices, too? Randi thought. She curled her toes into a ball. The skates squeezed her feet so tightly she could barely stand up.

She teetered to the right. She wobbled to the left. She grabbed for the boards at the edge of the ice.

Bam! She tripped and landed on her knees.

Anna skated over. "Are you okay?" she asked.

Randi got up quickly and brushed ice chips off her sweater. "I'm wearing Kate's skates," she whispered. "They're killing my feet!"

"Why don't you just tell Carol you lost your—"

"No!" Randi blurted out. "She might tell my mom. And Mom would be *so* mad at me for losing my skates! She's already mad that I can't find Kristi's library book and my purple panda shirt. I've got to pretend that everything's fine."

"Okay, kids," Carol called from the middle of the rink. "Let's go through the program for the competition."

Everyone in Figure Eights crowded around Carol. "Line up behind me," she instructed.

Randi went to the end of the line. She hoped Carol wouldn't pay much attention to whoever went last.

Carol began skating in a circle around the edge of the rink. Everyone in Figure Eights followed.

Inside Kate's too-small skates, Randi's toes felt like ten hot little potatoes. And they were getting hotter!

Please let me make it through practice, she thought.

Carol started off on a forward glide, followed by five forward strokes and five forward crossovers.

Randi did her best to complete the moves.

But it was hard. Her borrowed skates pinched like crazy. Her glide was really baby steps. Her crossovers didn't even cross over—she just moved her feet along, side by side.

I've got to do this! Randi thought.

Carol turned and slid into the backward crossovers.

Randi turned too. But while the rest of the Figure Eights did backward crossovers, Randi just took big, jerky steps.

"Now change to a one-foot glide!" Carol called. "Remember, keep your head up and your knees bent!"

Everybody in front of Randi lifted one foot. Randi lifted one foot too.

By now her pinched toes felt like ten sizzling-hot sausages! Randi's feet hurt so much she forgot everything she knew about the one-foot glide. She wobbled from side to side. She swung her arms in big circles.

She lurched forward. Her toe pick dug deep into the ice. Randi couldn't help it. She slammed straight into Woody!

"Watch it!" Woody yelled. He crashed onto the ice.

"Sorry," Randi called. She got her balance back. She pushed off with her right foot. But she was trying too hard. She skated too fast. She was out of control. And she was headed right for Samantha!

"Move, Samantha!" Randi cried.

Samantha didn't move fast enough.

Randi's skate clicked against Samantha's skate. Samantha stumbled and tripped. She landed flat on her bottom. "Yeouch!" she cried.

Randi glided right past her.

Woody was down. Samantha was down. Now Randi was headed toward Max. And gaining speed. She waved her arms in the air, but it didn't do any good.

"Out of my way, Max!" Randi shouted.

Max sped up, but Randi plowed straight into him. *Bam!* Down he went.

"Hey! What are you doing, Randi?" he yelled.

"It's my skates," Randi cried. "They're—"
Before she could finish her sentence—*wham!*

Randi slammed into Josh, who slammed into Frederika, who slammed into Anna.

Bam! Splat! Thunk!

One by one, they tumbled onto the ice.

Randi turned. And realized she was only two feet from the boards at the edge of the rink!

"Aaaaa!" she screamed.

Smack!

Randi plowed straight into the boards. She held on to the top of them tightly to keep from falling. Then she looked back across the ice.

Randi was the only skater still standing.

"Randi!" Carol exclaimed. "This is a disaster! Do you know how this happened? What got into you?"

It's not what got into me, Randi thought. *It's what my feet got into—borrowed skates!*

Randi looked up at Carol. "I don't exactly know what happened," she told her coach. "But I promise—it will never happen again."

8

Case Closed?

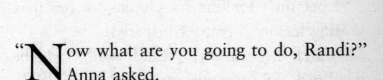

"Now what are you going to do, Randi?" Anna asked.

Two days after Randi's disaster at the rink, Randi was hanging out with Anna and Woody at Mr. Mullen's pro shop.

"I don't know anymore," Randi answered.

Randi was really worried. It was the day before the competition, and she still couldn't prove that Jessica had taken her skates.

Woody nudged Randi. "Hey, check out who just walked in."

Randi looked toward the door. She couldn't believe her eyes. *Jessica!*

"Quick! Hide!" Randi ordered.

Randi, Woody, and Anna ducked behind a tall set of shelves. The shelves were full of brand-new, expensive skates that Mr. Mullen had just set out on display.

"What is she doing here?" Woody asked.

Jessica wandered around the shop looking at sweaters, sweatshirts, and warm-up outfits.

"I bet she's looking for clothes for her new skating lessons," Anna whispered.

"Watch her closely," Randi said. "Maybe we'll pick up an important clue!"

Anna pressed her finger to her lips. "Listen! Jessica just asked my dad to show her the leotards."

Randi's eyes widened. She turned her head and listened to Mr. Mullen.

"They're right over here," Mr. Mullen answered Jessica. "I have a lot of different colors in your size."

Jessica picked up a bright blue leotard. "I like this one," she said. She carried the leotard over to the display case where Randi, Anna, and Woody were hiding!

That's when Randi noticed it—the bag slung over Jessica's shoulder. It looked like a skate bag.

Randi stared hard at the bag. She could tell there was something lumpy inside it. She felt a chill run through her.

Skates! Randi thought.

"I bet my skates are inside that bag right now," she whispered to Woody and Anna.

"Do you really think so?" Anna asked.

Randi narrowed her eyes at Jessica. "Yes, but I need to get a closer look."

Randi stepped onto the first shelf of the skate-display case. Then she climbed to the second, and the third. She peeked over the top of the case.

Jessica was still talking to Mr. Mullen. "All I have is a yucky old pair. I need new ones now that I'm starting lessons," Jessica said.

That's it! Randi thought. *That's all the proof*

I need! She's talking about getting new skates to replace my old skates! Well, I'm getting my skates back right now!

Randi began climbing back down the display case. But when she put out her foot, all she felt was air. Where was the shelf? Her foot waved around wildly. The display case swayed. It started to fall over.

"*Yeeeowwww!*" Randi yelled. The case crashed to the floor. Randi and fifty pairs of skates crashed with it. She landed right in front of Jessica!

Jessica jumped back. Mr. Mullen gasped and rushed over to Randi. Anna and Woody ran to Randi's side. Their eyes popped wide open.

"Are you okay, Randi?" they all asked.

"You bet I am!" Randi answered. She leaped to her feet, jumped over a pile of skates, and marched over to Jessica.

"What are you buying?" Randi demanded. "And what's in your skate bag?"

Jessica stared at Randi as if Randi were crazy. She placed her hands on her hips. "It's none of your business," she snapped. "But I'm buying things for my new ballet lessons. And my bag happens to be full of *books,* you big dummy!"

"Just as I thought—" Randi began. She gulped. "Did you say *books*? And *ballet* lessons?"

"Yes," Jessica told her. "I'm going to take ballet in the aerobics room here at the rink."

"But why were you looking at the new ice skates?" Randi asked.

"Ice skates?" Jessica frowned. "I wasn't looking at ice skates. I was looking for a new pair of tights, to go with this leotard," she said.

Randi realized that the display case full of skates stood right next to a rack of colorful tights.

"But—but then, where are my ice skates?" Randi asked in a tiny voice.

"Your ice skates? How would I know?" Jessica said. "Now *I* want to know why *you* were spying on me."

"Sp-Spying?" Randi stammered. She felt her

ears grow hot. "We weren't spying. We were just, uh, just curious about . . ." She glanced at Anna and Woody for help.

Both their faces were red. They turned and started quickly picking up the skates that had fallen onto the floor.

"Uh, we were just curious about your backpack," Randi told Jessica. "Yeah. That's it." She poked at the bag on Anna's back. "It's the coolest backpack we've ever seen. Right, Anna? Right, Woody?"

"Uh . . . right," they mumbled.

Jessica rolled her eyes. "You guys are too weird! Don't ever talk to me again! I'm leaving." She turned and marched out of the pro shop.

Randi's heart sank. She looked at her friends. "I guess maybe Jessica didn't steal my skates after all."

"I guess not," Anna said.

"We never had any *real* evidence," Randi admitted. "I'm sorry, guys. I got carried away. I thought Jessica did it, but I was wrong."

"We all thought Jessica took your skates, too," Woody said. "We're not such great detectives after all, are we?" he asked.

"Guess not," Anna said. She smiled. "Well, the good news is, Jessica's *not* a thief!"

Randi smiled back. Then she frowned. "But the bad news is, I still don't have my skates. And if Jessica didn't steal them, where are they?"

9

A Big Surprise!

"What a disaster!" Randi whispered to Big Six that night. Big Six was her teddy bear, a present from her parents for her sixth birthday. Randi told him all her secrets.

"I lost my skates, Big Six. I'm going to have to tell Mom about it. She'll be *so* angry. Plus, I messed up every practice. And my first competition is tomorrow. How can I win the competition and become a star like Jill when I don't even have any skates?"

Big Six stared at Randi with his big, brown button eyes.

Randi groaned. "How am I going to get out of this mess?"

"Did I hear something about a mess?"

Randi jumped at the sound of her mother's voice.

"I bet you were talking about your bedroom, Randi," Mrs. Wong said as she entered the room. She shook her head. "I asked you to clean your room days ago. I thought you were going to be more responsible, Randi. I thought you would clean up this room. No real skating champion would have a bedroom that looks as messy as this."

That's just it, Randi thought. *I'm not a real champion. I'm a real loser. I lost Jill's skates. And now I can't even be in the competition tomorrow. There's no way I can compete in someone else's skates.*

"I want you to clean up this room right now," Mrs. Wong said sternly. "And I'll be back to check on you." She turned and left the room.

"Guess I'd better get started," Randi grumbled to herself.

"Hey, Randi!"

Randi turned to see Kristi standing in the doorway. "Did you find my library book on jungle animals?"

Randi glanced nervously around the room. "Not yet."

Kristi rolled her eyes. "It's overdue, Randi. I'll be in big trouble if I don't bring it back to school tomorrow. And it will be all your fault."

"I'll find it. I promise," Randi told her sister.

"I hope so," Kristi said. She walked off down the hall.

Randi went right to work. She picked up a pair of shorts and put them in her dresser. Then she scurried around grabbing socks, T-shirts, sweaters, and jeans. She stuffed them in her drawers.

Next she hung up everything that was lying on her closet floor. "There. I put away my clothes. Now I'd better pick up the rest of this stuff," she told Big Six.

Randi picked up all her books, games, toys, and stuffed animals. She stacked them neatly on her shelves.

"Wow!" she cried when everything was put away. "I can see the floor again!"

"And doesn't it look nice!" Mrs. Wong said, poking her head back in the doorway. "You did a great job, Randi! But don't forget to clean under your bed."

"Okay," Randi said. She bent down to check under her bed. "Yikes! There's a ton of stuff under here!" she cried.

She pulled out a pair of jeans, her stuffed snake, a slipper, and her lost purple panda T-shirt! Now she and Anna could wear their shirts together after all!

Randi also found two pairs of leggings, one of Jill's skating magazines, and a library book with animals on the cover.

"Yes!" she cried. "Kristi's book!" Randi put the book on top of her bed. She could give it to Kristi later.

Randi crawled back under the bed. "There's

my sleeping bag. I don't believe it. Mom told me to put this in the laundry ages ago," she said to Big Six.

She sighed. "Mom is right—I haven't been very responsible with my things."

Randi pulled on the sleeping bag. She spotted something behind it. Something shiny.

She blinked and looked again.

Could it be? Was it possible?

She crawled closer and pushed the sleeping bag aside. There, sticking out from behind it, was a gold shoelace! Two gold shoelaces! Laces attached to white ice skates!

My skates! They were here all along! Randi couldn't believe it. *How could I have been so dumb!* she scolded herself. *I never took them to school at all! And my room was such a mess I didn't know they were here the whole time!*

She pulled out the skates. She hugged them to her chest and turned to face Big Six. "You heard it here first, Big Six," she said. "From now on, I'm going to keep my room clean. That's a promise!"

Randi looked at her skates. They were old, but they were beautiful to her.

"I can't wait to be in the competition now," she told Big Six. "I'm going to win! And Jill and I will both be ice-skating stars."

10

The Blue Ribbon

"**Y**ou're next, Randi," Carol called. "Are you ready?"

"Ready," Randi answered. She checked the gold laces in her skates one last time. She took a deep breath. And stepped onto the ice.

"Good luck," Anna whispered.

The bleachers were packed for the big competition. Randi's whole family sat in the front row, including little Laurie.

Everybody in Figure Eights had already skated. Everybody except Randi and Anna. *And they all made big mistakes,* Randi thought as she waited for the music to begin. *I won't make a mistake. Not with my skates.*

The music started. Randi glided perfectly into her forward and backward crossovers. Then she lifted her skate and slid into the one-foot glide. She remembered to keep her head up and her knees bent. She didn't wobble once. So far, she was skating a perfect program.

Now the bunny hop, she told herself. *Come on, skates! Don't let me down!*

Randi's skates didn't listen. As she pushed off on her left foot, Randi lost her balance and stumbled. Her toe pick dug into the ice.

She was falling! Then, somehow, she caught herself. She didn't fall. She got her balance back and glided smoothly into the bunny hop. She finished the program with a perfect hockey stop.

Everybody clapped and cheered. Randi beamed as she skated off the ice.

"That was great!" Anna whispered. "You made just one little mistake."

Randi felt really happy. She had skated the

best of anyone so far. She smiled as she imagined Jill pinning the blue ribbon on her skating dress.

"And now it's time for our final competitor," Carol announced. "Anna Mullen."

Randi watched as Anna took her position in the middle of the rink. When the music started, Anna glided easily into the forward and backward crossovers. Then she switched to the one-foot glide. She sailed across the rink on one skate. She didn't wobble once. She finished with a perfect bunny hop and a perfect hockey stop. Then she took a bow.

The audience clapped and shouted.

Before Carol announced it, Randi knew the truth. Anna had skated the whole program without one mistake! Anna had won!

Randi looked down at the ice. She didn't want anyone to see the tears that filled her eyes. Then suddenly Jill was standing by her side. She held the blue ribbon in her hand.

"I'm sorry you didn't win," Jill said. She put her arm around Randi. "What went wrong?"

Randi wiped her eyes. "Everything," she said. "Everything went wrong when I lost my skates."

"You lost your skates?" Jill repeated.

"Well, I didn't *really* lose them," Randi explained. "I just thought I did. And when I couldn't find them, I borrowed somebody else's. But those skates didn't fit, and I messed up at practice." She sighed. "I found *my* skates yesterday. But by then it was too late to practice." She stopped and looked up at her big sister. "I really wanted to win, Jill. I really wanted to get my picture in the paper with you. I wanted us to be ice-skating stars— together."

Jill wiped Randi's wet cheeks. "You tried your best, Randi," she said. "That's what really counts."

"But I was supposed to win!" Randi told Jill. "You won your first competition, and now you're a great skater. I *lost* my first competition. Now I'll never be as great as you!"

Jill smiled. "Even the greatest skaters don't win every competition."

"Even you?" Randi asked her big sister.

Jill wrapped her arm around Randi's shoulders. "Even me," she said. "And next time, if you work really hard, I know you can win." She grinned. "Especially if you practice in skates that fit!"

Jill leaned down and gave Randi a big hug. "Now I've got to go present the blue ribbon to Anna."

Randi watched Jill skate over to Anna. *Even if I didn't win, I'm glad my best friend did,* Randi thought.

Everybody cheered when Jill pinned the ribbon on Anna's sweater. A woman took their picture for the newspaper.

"Congratulations, Anna," Jill said. "You did a great job!"

"Ms. Wong!" the woman from the newspaper called. "Would you skate for us? One last time before you go to Colorado?"

The audience grew quiet, waiting for Jill's answer.

"Of course," Jill told the woman. "But since this is my last skate in Seneca Hills for a while, I'd like to do something special. I'd like to skate with my little sister Randi."

The audience cheered again. A huge grin broke out on Randi's face. She dashed across the ice to Jill.

"Hold it, you two," the newspaper woman called. "I want to get a picture of the famous Wong sisters."

Randi beamed. She smiled her biggest smile ever. The photographer snapped three pictures. *The Famous Wong Sisters are going to be in the newspaper together after all!* Randi thought.

Randi knew she was really going to miss Jill while she was away, but she also knew that if she practiced hard, she might go to the Ice Academy someday, too.

Then maybe Jill and Randi really *could* be the Famous Wong Sisters. Randi wrapped her arms around Jill and gave her a big hug.

"Come on, Randi," Jill said, hugging Randi back. "Everybody's waiting."

Jill straightened up, and Randi grasped her hand tightly.

The audience cheered as the two of them skated side by side around the ice.

About the Author

Effin Older is the author of many children's books published in the United States and abroad.

Effin lived in New Zealand for fourteen years. She currently lives in a tiny village in Vermont with her husband, Jules, and her white husky, Sophie. She has twin daughters named Amber and Willow.

When Effin isn't writing children's books, she likes to take long walks with Sophie, ride her mountain bike, and cross-country ski.

If you glided right through

jump into the SILVER BLADES series,
featuring Randi Wong's big sister Jill
and her friends.

Look for these titles at your bookstore or library: